What Kids Say About
Carole Marsh Mysteries . . .

I love the real locations! Reading the book always makes me want to go and visit them all on our next family vacation. My Mom says maybe, but I can't wait!

One day, I want to be a real kid in one of Ms. Marsh's mystery books. I think it would be fun, and I think I am a real character anyway. I filled out the application and sent it in and am keeping my fingers crossed!

History was not my favorite subject till I starting reading Carole Marsh Mysteries. Ms. Marsh really brings history to life. Also, she leaves room for the scary and fun.

I think Christina is so smart and brave. She is lucky to be in the mystery books because she gets to go to a lot of places. I always wonder just how much of the book is true and what is made up. Trying to figure that out is fun!

Grant is cool and funny! He makes me laugh a lot!

I like that there are boys and girls in the story of different ages. Some mysteries I outgrow, but I can always find a favorite character to identify with in these books.

They are scary, but not too scary. They are funny. I learn a lot. There is always food which makes me hungry. I bet like I am there!

What Parents and Teachers Say About Carole Marsh Mysteries . . .

I think kids love these books because they have such a wealth of detail. I know I learn a lot reading them! It's an engaging way to look at the history of any place or event. I always say I'm only going to read one chapter to the kids, but that never happens—it's always two or three, at least!
—Librarian

Reading the mystery and going on the field trip—Scavenger Hunt in hand—was the most fun our class ever had! It really brought the place and its history to life. They loved the real kids characters and all the humor. I loved seeing them learn that reading is an experience to enjoy!
—4th grade teacher

Carole Marsh is really on to something with these unique mysteries. They are so clever; kids want to read them all. The Teacher's Guides are chock full of activities, recipes, and additional fascinating information. My kids thought I was an expert on the subject—and with this tool, I felt like it!
—3rd grade teacher

My students loved writing their own Real Kids/Real Places mystery book! Ms. Marsh's reproducible guidelines are a real jewel. They learned about copyright and more & ended up with their own book they were so proud of!
—Reading/Writing Teacher

"The kids seem very realistic—my children seemed to relate to the characters. Also, it is educational by expanding their knowledge about the famous places in the books."

"They are what children like: mysteries and adventures with children they can relate to."

"Encourages reading for pleasure."

"This series is great. It can be used for reluctant readers, and as a history supplement."

The Secret of SK LLCRACKER SWAMP

by Carole Marsh

Published by Gallopade International/Carole Marsh Books. Printed in the
United States of America.

Managing Editor: Sherry Moss
Cover Design: Michele Winkelman
Illustrations: Brittany Donaldson, Savannah College of Art & Design
Content Design: Steven St. Laurent, Line Creek Creative

Gallopade International is introducing SAT words that kids need to know in
each new book that we publish. The SAT words are bold in the story. Look for
this special logo beside each word in the glossary. Happy Learning!

Gallopade is proud to be a member and supporter of these educational organizations and
associations:

American Booksellers Association
American Library Association
International Reading Association
National Association for Gifted Children
The National School Supply and Equipment Association
The National Council for the Social Studies
Museum Store Association
Association of Partners for Public Lands
Association of Booksellers for Children

This book is a complete work of fiction. All events are fictionalized, and although the
names of real people are used, their characterization in this book is fiction.

a Word from the author

Dear Reader,

My granddaughter, Christina, and I like to speculate on "What if?" As you may know, I write mysteries set in real places that feature real kids as characters. The story is made up (fiction), but the fascinating historic facts are true (non-fiction). We are both often amused when readers guess "backwards" about what I made up and what is true in the books. Sometimes, I have a hard time being sure myself! Why? Because history is just as interesting and incredible as anything an author can make up.

So, one day, Christina and I were wondering: "What if a big city girl, who had never spent much time with her great-outdoors father, went to stay with him as he worked in the wild and wooly Okefenokee Swamp? It was easy to imagine a story that could be interesting, funny, scary, and feel real. But the truth is, the "Land of Trembling Earth," as the Okefenokee Swamp was called by the Indians, has so much flabbergasting history that you have a big head start on a great story, no matter what you write about!

As I told Christina about the real swamp...its fascinating history of swampers who learned to survive there...the threats to the swamp's survival...and the snakes, alligators, and mosquitoes "as big as dinner plates"—not to mention the snakes!—well, it all seemed Pretty Darn Scary. I hope you, and Christina, think so, too!

Carole Marsh

Pretty Darn Scary Books in This Series

table of Contents

PROLOGUE

RECEIPTS AND REMEDIES

Tabby was curled up in the canvas tent reading an 1800s-era book of "receipts and remedies."

For Mosquito Bites:
Wet salt into a paste with a little vinegar and rub on the bites to stop itching.

To Stop Bleeding:
Compress old cobwebs into a lump and apply to the wound, or use the insides of freshly-broken eggshells.

If Struck by Lightning:
Stand in a cold water shower for two hours.

For Diarrhea:
Drink blackberry wine.   Drink blackberry tea.   Eat blackberries.

The only thing Tabby could find no cure for was being bored to death, dying of lonesomeness, or...being eaten alive by an alligator.

CHAPTER ONE

SKULLCRACKER SWAMP

Tabby hunkered down in the canvas tent, squatted, squirmed, and performed other gyrations to pull on her white cut-off jeans and a brown tee shirt with boot prints on the back that read: TAKE A HIKE.

Sure, she thought as she squiggled into the jeans and tried to zip them while hovering on her knees and bending backwards; the tent was a small one-person pop-up job. *Sure, hike in a swamp; get eaten alive.*

Tabby was a city girl. She had grown up in Atlanta, Georgia—the City of the South, the Phoenix that Rose from the Ashes. She had lived with her grandmother in a modern condo practically at the crossroads of the famous Peachtree Street and Ponce de Leon Avenue. The fabulous Fox Theater was nearby, a Persian gem of a castle where her grandmother took her to Broadway performances, ballets, and to see *Gone With the Wind* on the giant movie screen. The marquee out front, lit up in colorful neon lights, actually gave her goosebumps.

But the goosebumps she got in this swamp were a different matter entirely. She was living with her dad this summer. He was a Swampmaster, or something like that, she'd call it. It was worse than being the daughter of Crocodile Dundee or Animal Planet's Alligator Guy, or whatever he called himself.

Actually, her father was a professor and famous for his environmental efforts regarding swamps and saving them from destruction. Tabby just wished he'd do it without her. She loved him, but really, was this any way to spend a summer? Hunkered down in a squat, smelly tent? Swatting mosquitoes the size of saucers? Sweating to beat the band? No friends except frogs...and she did NOT like frogs. Nothing to do but wait for Dad to get back from that day's journey into the hinterlands of the swamp to do who-knew-what?

"Have fun!" he'd say merrily, as he tramped off. "Explore! I'll be back at sunset and we'll have a feast!"

Of course, Tabby was afraid to explore. She was not having any fun at all. And her father's idea of a feast was roast possum or some other critter he'd nabbed in the swamp.

It was a nightmare, she thought. This summer was a nightmare. Not only did she fear that she would not survive it, she was not even sure that she wanted to survive it. It didn't help that the never-ending swath of weeds and water which surrounded them was nicknamed "Skullcracker Swamp" by her father and his long-time swamp friend, Mable. It was pretty darn scary here.

Suddenly, Tabby heard a creaking, the snap of twigs, and the heavy fall of footsteps. Trembling, she unzipped the tent a few inches and poked her head out. It was her Dad, coming ashore in his little boat, traipsing through the wet grass toward her like Indiana Bones, as she had secretly nicknamed him.

"Hey," he greeted her with a grin. "Look what I brought for dinner!"

Tabby's father held up one fat, dead armadillo. Tabby pulled her head back inside the tent, rezipped it angrily, and fell down onto a rough tarp.

She began to cry.

CHAPTER TWO

SWAMPMASTER

"Uh, Dad..." Tabby began. "I don't think I can eat something that looks like a big, brown bug."

Professor Flynn held the slumping armadillo aloft with one hand and shoved his hat back on his head with the other. "Oh, I don't mean this!" he promised his daughter. "I just wanted you to see this big guy—isn't he fascinating!?"

Tabby nodded but she didn't mean it. The pathetic dead critter looked like something from Jurassic Park with his paint chip-looking plates hanging limply over his body. His long snout and long tail made her think *rodent*. She wondered how many of these things she usually thought of only as "road kill" were scampering around in the swamp.

Her Dad tossed the armadillo aside and pulled a paper sack out of the boat. Tabby cringed as he reached inside and grabbed a plastic bag and yanked it out and handed it to her. She feared what might be inside.

"Two big T-bone steaks, two humongous baked potatoes, a head of lettuce, and tomatoes for my girl," the professor said proudly. "I caught an air boat ride over to the market at Fargo. Thought we could do with a hearty meal tonight." He turned to the chore of securing his boat.

Tabby unzipped the tent all the way and poked her head out. She grabbed the sack and clutched it to her chest. "Food!" she squealed happily. "Real food! Thank goodness!" They had lived on peanut butter and jelly and slightly molded bread and dried chipped beef on the same moldy bread for days.

The professor just shook his head. "Fire up the grill!" he said. "We'll eat it all for dinner." He was not used to being around his daughter, and he knew she did not want to be here, but he wanted to please her in every way he could.

It pleased him immensely to finally see her smile...a smile that instantly faded to a frown of fear as they both heard from the swamp a loud...

ROAR!!

CHAPTER THREE

THE ROAR!

Even in broad daylight, the sound that Tabby and her father heard was petrifying!

Tabby had no idea what the sound was, or could be—surely not something of this earth. Or maybe it was something not from this era. The humongous roar had actually made the earth tremble! The dramatic sound was made even more startling by arising out of the beautiful, blue sky morning. Indeed, in spite of herself, even Tabby had noted that the blue sky, white puppy clouds, lime green of the swamp grasses, and sweet smells of blooming wildflowers had caught her by surprise.   But this sound...this horrible sound...was most surprising of all.

While Tabby had frozen in place at the roar, blond bangs waving wisps in the sun, her father did not move, did not blink.   She stared at him listening so intently. For the first time, she felt like she understood just what a swampmaster he was.   Although he did not move, she could see, could feel him assessing the sound and what it meant with all his senses.

Surely through his eyes, ears, and the very pores of his skin, he had an inkling of not only the source of the roar, but the location, and, perhaps, the reason.   His mind, she felt, was flipping through research tomes, scientific data, and anything else he had ever read or learned, to try to fathom the secret of the roar.

At last he spoke, softly.   "Bull alligator.   Monster size for sure.   Maybe near Harpers Hammock.   But why?" he wondered aloud.   "Something disturbed the Old Man, surely."

And from then on, the giant male alligator was referred to by them as the Old Man.   "I heard the Old Man," her dad might say, upon returning from his daily swamp chores.   "Did the Old Man get it?" Tabby had asked when her father had lost a shoe.   It was their private joke and the beginning of a new relationship, the kind of relationship when a daughter realizes that her father is more than just a Dad, and a father understands that his little girl is growing up and becoming her own independent woman.

But on this morning, the professor just said, "I'll check it out later; it seems very suspicious to me." His daughter could not tell that he was just teasing her.

"Scared?" Tabby had teased. She did not joke much with her Dad, so he gave her a curious look.

"No, hungry," he said. "Are you just gonna wave that bag around till a gator grabs it or are we going to eat?" Tabby could not tell if he was teasing or angry, so she hurried to build a fire—at least one thing she'd learned in Girl Scouts that had helped her so far here in the famous, dreadful (to her) Okefenokee Swamp.

CHAPTER FOUR

OLD MAN

The steaks were delicious! The potatoes were even better; the professor had had his daughter rub the outside with coarse salt before cooking them in the coals of the fire she had built. Even the lettuce and tomato salad, with no dressing but the blood-red juice, was scrumptious.

After dinner, Tabby and her father sat near the gray coal eyes of the fire and watched the swamp go to sleep.

"It *is* beautiful, Dad," Tabby admitted. "But sometimes, it is so scary, like when that bull alligator roared this afternoon."

"I understand, Tabitha," her father said, using her given name like a pet name. He always said it when he wanted to be kind or sweet or understanding, unlike some parents who say their child's given name when they are calling them to task for not minding. "TAB-ITH-AH!" her grandmother used to holler when she got aggravated with the small child she had not planned to raise in her old age.

Tabby's mother had run off to California to be an artist when Tabby was still in preschool. She had found being married to someone as serious and hard-working as Tabby's dad "boring." Tabby figured she must have found being a mother boring, too, because one day, she just dropped her off at her Grammy Martha's and never came back.

Dad had been away at school that year, finishing his college degree in botany. Tabby guessed that he must have been depressed, or maybe in shock, because when he graduated, he did not come home. He went straight back to school for his masters degree, then got his doctorate. Tabby figured he must have taken a gazillion classes in weird stuff ranging from swamp biology to historic chemistry, and who knows what.

Holidays found him on far-off research trips; summers he was gone on long teaching assignments or working on one of the many books he had written. He was pretty famous in his field, but he was a stranger to his daughter, and she to him.

When Grammy Martha had died, the professor found that he finally had to be a real dad, or try. And Tabby found her big city life flushed into a world of water, wiregrass, bug bites, and things that holler and go bump in the night.

She was trying to make the best of this first week. But, really, the summer was already beginning to seem like one long, pretty darn scary nightmare. She wished that school was starting tomorrow! And, even then, she was not sure what school, where, or when. Her future was as uncertain as the pink-glowing horizon where the jagged silhouette of spiky grass looked like black teeth chowing down on the little daylight left in the sky.

"I wonder where Old Man is tonight?" her dad said.

"Why did he make such a noise?" Tabby asked with a shiver.

"That's how big, giant alligators sound," the professor answered. "It's a sound like no other, that's for sure. Something must have greatly upset him. It's mating season, you know. Maybe another alligator was after his girl?"

Tabby giggled. "So how many gators are there in this swamp?" she bravely inquired.

Her dad gave her a "look" with his ocean blue eyes from beneath his long black eyelashes. "I don't think you want to know," he said. "But remember, it wasn't all that long ago, when alligators here were on the endangered list. For years, people killed them for their hides, which they sold to be made into purses and boots and belts and jackets. Even after killing them was banned, poachers kept at it. But, boy, when the gators made a comeback, they made a big one!"

Tabby nodded. She had seen a local paper when they came through Waycross that showed pictures of alligators from Florida to Virginia "interacting" with the local people. Some gators lazed on golf courses. One picture showed an alligator near Hilton Head standing up beside the front door of a house, as if it was about to ring the doorbell. Another gator was shown climbing a chain link fence. The article talked about how many people, children, or small pets had been snatched, and often killed, by alligators.

"Dad, do you think we're gonna get out of here alive?" Tabby asked. She was serious.

Her father laughed. "Tabby," he said, "I promise that by the time the summer is over and you go back to school that you will have learned to love the swamp. In fact, you'll want to come back next year."

"Dad, I don't think so!"

"Well, we'll see," said Dad. "But tomorrow, now that we're settled, I'll take you out in the boat with me and start your swamp education."

"Is it safe?" Tabby asked.

"Of course!" the professor answered.

Tabby looked out at the swamp, which she could only faintly see. Suddenly, the swamp came alive with rising fireflies. It looked as if fairy fireworks were putting on a show from the ground up. It was beautiful...amazing...and quite a surprise.

So was the next thing they heard: Old Man growling a loud goodnight. *And he sounded much closer.*

CHAPTER FIVE

LAND OF THE TREMBLING EARTH

The next morning, sure enough, they headed out into the swamp. It was a day Tabby would never forget, nor forgive her father for.

They got up early, before dawn. Dad said *that* was when a botanist's day began. Tabby figured it would do no good to remind him that girls out of school for the summer often liked to sleep in late.

She found it confusing and frustrating to "break camp" in the darkness. But before they were done strapping their tents and other camping gear on the back of the small boat, pink light began to seep up out of the swamp and meet the sky that appeared to slide down to meet it like a large blue window shade.

"It's gonna be hot," Dad said, shoving them off the bank.

"What else is new?" Tabby answered, slapping a mosquito trying to devour her shoulder for its breakfast.

"It'll be cooler out on the water," Dad said as the boat moved silently through the narrow corridor of creek. Tabby peered at the map. She was supposed to navigate. *Fat chance*, she thought, since she didn't know north from south from east from west. Luckily, as the sky brightened, she spotted a compass rose in the corner of the map and shifted the paper to try to orient herself to the direction that she thought they were headed.

For a while they moved through the looking glass water in silence. But as Tabby began to listen to the silence, she heard many sounds. The swamp was active in the morning. Birds tweeted and twittered. Bankside brush rustled. Twigs *cricked* overhead. Something moaned. Another thing howled. A woodpecker *rat-a-tatted*. Even the slight breeze inhaled and exhaled audibly across the swamp.

Soon, Dad began to softly identify the sounds: "Chuck-will's-widow...little tree frog...coot..." And as they began to spy wildlife on the move: "Jackdaw...the Preacher...joree...sapsucker."

Tabby couldn't get over how primeval the swamp seemed to her, as if it had been here for all time, unbothered, untamed, minding its own business—an idea that she would later learn was completely untrue, for the swamp was geologically "young."

Suddenly, out of a mass of maidencane where another canal cut into the waterway they were on, an air boat appeared. It whipped around in a tight circle, blasting them with the wind and waterspray from its huge fan. It *whooshed* right to a stop in front of them; its wake rocked their small boat. Tabby clenched her hands tightly to the sides until the boat settled down.

"Holler at me, professor!" an odd-shaped and wrinkle-faced woman roared across their bow.

Professor Flynn laughed back and gave the woman a wave. "You about scared us to death, Mable! Was that an intentional attack or are you in a hurry for breakfast?"

Tabby was stunned that his father knew this strange woman with the wild hair and eerie green eyes. The term *Swamp Thing* came to her mind.

"Had breakfast hours ago!" the woman screeched back. "Just down the crick there tryin' to trap me some lunch. Didn't hear you two comin' along. Who's the gal?"

Mable asked this as if Tabby were some specimen that the professor had plucked from the swamp and was hauling back to base camp.

"My daughter, Tabitha," the professor said proudly, waving his arm toward the back of the boat. "Say good morning to 'Aunt' Mable Harper, honey," he commanded. "She's a real swamper!"

Tabby only nodded. She continued to think her own private thoughts—including that hopefully she was *not related to this "!"*

Her dad went on. "Mable's lived in the swamp all her life. *Looks like it!* She's a great hunter, fisher, and trapper. *Smells like it!* Was my guide and companion my first research trip here." *Really, Dad!* A vanishing breed! *Not soon enough.*

Mable blushed and frowned. "Don't think your daughter is impressed, professor. Maybe she needs to come along with me and learn a little swamp self-reliance?" The woman let out a wild laugh.

Tabby cringed. She grabbed her dad by his arm and found her voice. "No, Dad, really! I'd rather stay with you today, please? Please?"

But her father looked immensely pleased by the woman's invitation. "Great idea, Mable!" he said. "I'll bet Tabby could use some female companionship after sticking with me all week."

Tabby thought she might faint. But her father was oblivious to her stress and discomfort. *"Pleeeeease?"* she begged.

But he was already helping to gather her things and pass them across the bow of his boat to Mable. "It'll be fun," he promised. Another swamp experience to add to your 'What I did on my summer vacation' essay when school starts back. What say?"

Tabby did not answer her dad, but just gave him a peck on the cheek and climbed over the bow of their boat and into the woman's boat, trying not to get bladed to death by the air boat's fan.

Before she was hardly in, Mable *whooshed* off through the swamp with a wave back to the professor and hollered, "See ya at dusk!"

What I did on my summer vacation–DIE! thought Tabby.

CHAPTER SIX

MABLE, THE SWAMP THING

Tabby held on to the sides of the boat for dear life and the wild woman hollered and laughed crazily as she sped the air boat in a zigzag pattern through the swamp waterways. It was frightening, but in a way, Tabby thought, it was fun—like some amusement park ride, only no other kids were there to enjoy it with her...and she had no idea where they were going or when they would stop rocking and rolling along the water.

At last, Mable *ka-whooshed* the boat to a halt under the shade of a tall bald cypress tree. She tied up to a cypress knee and pulled a croker sack out from beneath one of the boat seats.

"Might as well have lunch right here," she said, tugging open the sack.

Tabby cringed, wondering what swamp stuff she would be offered for lunch; she felt like she might throw up. Mable thrust a paper-wrapped *something* at her and Tabby giggled when she reluctantly opened it and discovered that it was a peanut butter and jelly sandwich.

Mable winked at her. "Thought it was raw armadillo, didn't you?" she teased. Then she surprised Tabby yet again by tossing her an ice-cold Dr. Pepper out of a white foam cooler.

"Thanks," Tabby said, really meaning it. She was starving and this "real food" seemed like a feast. She actually relaxed as she sat back against the boat's transom and bit into her sandwich. When she felt something lumpy, and pulled out a round, black thing, she squinted.

"Raisins," said Mable, with another wink. "Good for ya. Get 'em at the grocery at Folkston. Man don't live by swamp food alone, you know?"

Tabby laughed in spite of herself. Aunt Mable was a real character. "Have you really lived in the Okefenokee   all   your   life?"   she   asked.

Mable nodded. "Born a tadpole on a toadstool, I reckon. My people's buried in a graveyard on one island where I live. Love the Suwannee River...seen great fires destroy a lot of forest...hunkered down in hurricanes in the heart of the swamp. Witnessed grudges and murders. Done business with bear, cougar, rattler, and gator." The woman raised her skirt to show a long, jagged scar on the calf of her leg. "Anybody think a swamp's boring hasn't spent any time in one."

Tabby chewed and nodded. She had never thought about it that way. "Do you have any family?"

The woman looked far off to the western horizon, as if to see if she had any family standing and waving to her out that way. Slowly, she shook her head. "Was married once. Met Oba at a swamp frolic. Had two kids. Oba died...kids moved away...I stayed."

"Why? Aren't you lonely?" asked Tabby, not meaning to be nosy, but curious why the old woman lived alone in the swamp when she had family, maybe even grandchildren Tabby's age.

Mable smiled. "Cause the Okefenokee's the most beautiful place in the world. And if you think I live all alone out here, just look behind you."

Tabby turned just in time to see an enormous water moccasin weave its way through the cypress knees and snug up right beside their boat!

CHAPTER SEVEN

SKULLCRACKER SWAMP

After lunch, Aunt Mable fired up the air boat and they headed on through the blue and green of the amazingly endless marsh. Just as Dad had (only roaring loudly), Mable pointed and named swamp stuff as they sailed along: "Hammock...live oaks...Spanish moss...Grand Prairie...Buzzard Roost Lake..." and finally, as she silenced the air boat to a stop, "Skullcracker Swamp: home sweet home."

Tabby wondered why anyone would want to live in a place called Skullcracker Swamp. Truly, the small island hammock looked haunted with its forest of long-armed live oak trees draped with gray beards of Spanish moss. Only when a breeze parted the limbs did enough sunlight scamper through the leaves to light up the ancient tin roof of the cracker shack that was Aunt Mable's home.

It would feel like Halloween all the time, Tabby thought. Trick-or-treaters might be bats, snakes, spiders, and who knows what else!? Tabby shivered.

"Don't be afyeard," Aunt Mable said and Tabby realized that her curious lingo meant *afraid*.

"I'm not," Tabby lied, as she jumped out of the boat and sat on a mottled brown and green rock while the old woman secured the boat.

"I swear, I'm all in," Aunt Mable said with a sigh; she wiped her brow with a dirty rag.

Tabby was confused, but assumed the woman meant not that she was still in the boat but that she was worn out from getting up so early and fishing and hunting, or whatever she had been doing out there in the swamp.

"Can I help you out?" Tabby asked. And as she started to get up, the rock beneath her moved. She jumped up with a screech, then blushed as she saw the large turtle "rock" she had been sitting on slowly amble toward the water!

She felt so stupid; how could a city girl like her know anything about a swamp or its inhabitants? When Aunt Mable roared with laughter, it made Tabby angry.

But when she looked at the woman, she saw that she was not laughing at Tabby's ignorance, but just enjoying a moment of joy in the swamp. Tabby just brushed the back of her cut-offs, grabbed a croker sack Aunt Mable thrust at her, and headed for the shack.

"You can plop it there," Aunt Mable said, indicating the croker sack.

Tabby dropped it on the porch. When she did, something about the flutter sound inside made her realize that the sack was not filled with boating gear, but with an animal of some sort.

Aunt Mable helped Tabby wipe the quizzical look from her face by yanking the sack from the bottom and shaking it. At Tabby's feet—indeed, across her bare toes—flopped a dead opossum. "Dinner," she said and vanished indoors behind a slammed screened door.

Skullcracker Swamp, indeed, thought Tabby, who suddenly felt as if her own skull were cracking half in two.

CHAPTER EIGHT

THE SECRET

Tabby gingerly sucked her toes out from under the gray fur of the "possum" and backed away. Forlornly, she sat on the top step of the log cabin's porch. Just when she was certain that she couldn't feel worse, she had a horrible thought: *What if Dad did not come back for her? What if he forgot? Or got lost? Or eaten by a gator? Or maybe was tired of a bored girl who did not share his enthusiasm for the great, grisly outdoors?*

This was her state of mind when Aunt Mable suddenly reappeared with a surprise Tabby could actually relish: two tall glasses of homemade lemonade, complete with ice. Tabby rewarded her captor with a sincere smile. At least I won't die of thirst, she thought, wondering if the old woman was what Dad referred to as "addled," meaning plumb crazy!

To Tabby's surprise, Aunt Mable sat across from her on the top step. She leaned into the sagging pillar with a tired sigh. "Want to hear a secret?" she asked.

Now, Tabby was stumped. Aunt Mable did not seem like the kind of person who shared her sorrows or her secrets. Surely, she was the most self-reliant person Tabby had ever met, somehow surviving out here in thousands of acres of wild swamp with no phone, no car, and no friends (Tabby guessed) but unfriendly varmints.

"Sure," Tabby said, "I can keep a secret." She smiled at the old woman.

Aunt Mable frowned. "I didn't say you had to keep it. You may have to help me solve it."

"What is your secret?" Tabby asked, now curious. And, she wondered, how do you "solve" a secret?

Aunt Mable frowned again. "I didn't say it was *my* secret," she said grumpily. "I said it was *a* secret. It's someone else's secret; that's why it needs solving."

"Like a mystery?" asked Tabby, wondering how she could help solve any mystery that might be made up of secrets in a swamp.

For a long time, Aunt Mable was quiet, as if perhaps reconsidering sharing the secret. At last, she sighed. "I know you don't know much about the swamp," she began. "You probably think the swamp is peaceful and quiet except for the critters and varmints that inhabit it. And, mostly, it is."

Aunt Mable adjusted her long skirt and shifted her shoulders the way Tabby's granddad had done when his arthritis bothered him. It was only then that Tabby realized just how old the old lady really was. Maybe 70? Even 80?

"But the swamp is a living thing in many ways," she went on, as if she had never stopped talking. "Plenty of people and action here at one time or another. First the Indians—Timucuans and Creek a'fightin'. Then the Spanish explorers; they couldn't tame this swamp and moved on! The Indians and the homesteaders fought. Some folks tried to drain the swamp and grow crops—what a folly! Some folks tried to cut all the wood out of the swamp for lumber or turpentine. If it isn't man a'pesterin' the swamp, it's nature. Droughts let the fires come. It's a wonder the swamp survives!"

Tabby was puzzled. "But Dad said that President Franklin Roosevelt made the Okefenokee a national wildlife refuge...that it's a protected wilderness."

Aunt Mable *harrumphed*. "As long as there's anything of value in the swamp, people will try to get to it—no matter what they destroy."

Tabby looked out at the mirrorlike water, the many hues of colors from gray to green to blue. For a moment she could actually agree that it was the most beautiful place on earth. "But what's the secret?"

Aunt Mable looked old, tired, and sad. "The secret, and the mystery, is why would someone want to destroy me? If they'll just wait, I'll die of pure natural causes and then they can get to whatever I'm a-sleeping on that they would kill for."

Kill for, Tabby repeated in her mind. *Kill for!?* She looked out at the islands of cypress trees and tall stands of pine. She felt as if eyes were watching her...and the eyes did not belong to an animal, *but a human being.*

CHAPTER NINE

SWAMP FROLIC

That night, Tabby had one of the most shocking events of the summer so far: she had fun!

Dad finally showed up at dusk, just in time for them all to sit on the porch and watch the swamp chug down the giant orange ball of sun.

Mable was thrilled to have company and had set out a swamp feast. Although Tabby had feared fried possum, they actually had chicken, vegetables, homemade biscuits, cane syrup, and huckleberry pie.

All through dinner, Mable and the professor talked about old times. Tabby was surprised to find that she enjoyed hearing their tall tales. "If history was this interesting in school, I sure would be more interested in history," she confessed.

"Some things just don't end up in a textbook," Dad agreed. "Too bad. Most of the really interesting history is about people and their shenanigans. Blood and guts. Trials and tribulations. Murder and mayhem."

Aunt Mable shook her head in animated agreement. "I think swamp history is best found in scars...scars on the land, scars on the body and even the soul, and in memories—good-uns and bad."

After dinner, Aunt Mable sipped a dark liquid from a little cup. Dad whispered behind his hand to his daughter, "Moonshine!" The old woman giggled. Tabby pretended to be shocked.

Her dad finally talked Tabby into taking a sip of the swamp water he was drinking. She was shocked to discover that it was actually quite sweet and delicious.

After a few more sips from the little cup, Aunt Mable pulled out a harmonica and played and sang (very off key!) old swamp tunes with names like *Young Soldier Boy* and *Backwards from Ten*. "I sung this one at the ought-four frolic," she'd say, then plough right into another tune.

As the night wore on, Tabby dozed off in a hammock on the porch, only occasionally lifting a limp wrist to swat at a buzzing mosquito. But she was not so sound asleep that she did not overhear her father and the old woman talking. She was telling him the secret.

"But who would want to bother you?" the professor asked.

"I don't know," the old woman responded in a tired voice. "But they better beware my battlin' stick," she said with determination.

"Oh, they're in trouble now," Dad teased her. But even in near-sleep, Tabby could tell that her father's laugh was just to ease Aunt Mable's mind. She was surprised that she could tell that about her father since they had spent so little time together. She thought it was sweet that he was so kind to the old woman, and had somehow known that it would be good for Tabby to spend some time with her.

Just as she was having these pleasant thoughts, she peeked open her eyes to see an enormous golden moon rise from the swamp. She thought that it was the most magical thing that she had ever seen.

When she closed her eyes to seek pleasant dreams, the last thing she overheard was Aunt Mable saying: "I think it was good we didn't tell Miss Tabby that chicken was really gator, don't you?"

At that moment, Old Man let out a prehistoric roar so loud that the earth did tremble, and neither of the two adults—busy staring up at the moon—heard Tabby tip out of her hammock and throw up over the side of the porch!

CHAPTER TEN

BUGABOO ISLAND

Dad woke Tabby up at dawn. She had a sour stomach. Much to her surprise, Aunt Mable snored loudly as she slept on through their preparations to take the boat out into the swamp.

Tabby caught Dad give the old woman a tender look. Then his face altered to an expression of worry and concern.

"Come on," he whispered to his daughter, "Let's go."

Tabby was a little bothered and surprised that they didn't say goodbye or leave a note, but when she asked her father about that, he just smiled. "Swampers don't need no notes," he said, chucking his gear into the boat and holding it steady for Tabby to get in.

"Dad!" Tabby teased. "Don't talk so illiterately! You're a professor, you know." She crawled in the boat, her knuckles not quite as white today as she held to the sides.

Her dad laughed. "Cain't help it," he said. "I get down here in these swamp parts, and I jest tend to take on the vernacular."

"The what?" Tabby asked as they shoved off.

"You, know," Dad said, "the local dialect. It's pretty unique."

"Yeah," said Tabby with a laugh. "Sometimes, I could hardly understand Aunt Mable." When she told me she was 'out of chat' I finally figured out she meant that she didn't have anything else to talk about."

"Well, that's rare!" said Dad, poling the boat out of the reeds so he could start the motor.

"Did she tell you her 'secret'?" Tabby asked quietly. Aunt Mable had not said she could not tell; besides, maybe her father could help.

The professor looked worried. "Yes, she did. But you know, I don't know if she's serious or just imagining things. You can get a pretty wild imagination in the swamp. Maybe she's just getting old, but I'm not taking any chances. Our project today is not botany, it's search and rescue."

"Huh?" said Tabby.

"We're going to do a little reconnaissance to see if we can solve the mystery of whether Mable's truly in danger or not," Dad explained.

"And how do we do that?" asked Tabby, looking around at the endless swamp.

Her father chuckled. "You still don't get it, do you? This swamp is not the forlorn land you think it is...it's living, breathing, and more active than you can imagine. And that includes human activity—good and bad."

Without another word, the professor turned and started the quiet, little motor and their small, silvery boat slithered through the watercourse as smoothly as a lazy snake.

In a moment, he called back over his shoulder to his daughter: "We're headed to Bugaboo Island."

CHAPTER ELEVEN

WAY DOWN UPON THE SUWANNEE RIVER, FAR FAR AWAY

Tabby had anticipated a leisurely ride through the Okefenokee that still and quiet morning, but it seemed it was one small adventure after another.

For awhile, she just sat back in the boat and enjoyed the scenery. Sometimes she caught her reflection in the tea-colored water and wondered if she looked happy or sad, scared or satisfied.

As they moved through the vast wilderness, they heard the raucous call of the sandhill crane, frogs croaked, and Dad pointed out gator holes as they passed them.

Suddenly, the water churned up ahead. Tabby just knew an alligator was going to pop up out of the froth.

Instead, a large blob of brown matter burst to the surface.

"What's that!?" she squealed.

"Peat," said her father, steering around the mess. "The swamp makes vegetation faster than it can rot. The decayed vegetation sinks to the bottom and decomposes, producing methane gas. When enough gas builds up, it explodes the mat of peat up to the surface of the water."

"So I see!" said Tabby.

"Actually," said her father, "that's what you're standing on when you're on an 'island' in the swamp—a peat bog that grows, gets vegetated, and eventually becomes land you can walk on...even though it's actually floating. So it's no wonder the Indians called the Okefenokee the *Land of Trembling Earth*."

"Well, the place is certainly full of surprises," Tabby agreed.

Tabby's next surprise was to see a bug get eaten by a plant! When they stopped for lunch, her father pointed out a hooded pitcher plant, a bladderwort, a sundew, and a golden trumpet. She didn't quite catch on when he explained that these plants were **"carnivorous."**

As he dug out lunch from the cooler while he talked, Tabby stared at a plant with a long, tubular flower. An insect circled the flower once or twice, then dove into the tube. Tabby looked into the tube and saw the bug trapped in a liquid that filled the bottom.

When her dad turned and saw his daughter

staring into the plant, he asked, "What part of carnivorous didn't you understand?" With a twinkle in his eye, he explained how these plants lured, trapped, and ate insects to survive.

"At least I'm bigger than they are!" said Tabby, making a mental note: *Keep your hands inside the boat at all times!*

After lunch, they saw a white ibis with its orange curved bill and orange legs wading in the water...enormous osprey nests sprawled atop dead trees like a bad hair-do...graceful blue herons floating through the sky...vultures chowing down on a dead raccoon...an eagle soaring overhead...a funny otter peeking up at them as he lay on his back in the water...and ducks—bottoms up!—flapping their funny webbed feet in the air as they fed.

Tabby was certain that no zoo or aquarium was quite as miraculous as this. She was feeling pretty happy, until an iridescent rainbow snake skidded by. She yelped and so did her father, grabbing his camera.

"That's such a rare sight!" he said. Tabby thought he would tip the boat over trying to get a shot of the black snake with red stripes and yellow belly.

But the real adventure came at midafternoon. Surprisingly to Tabby, they came upon a swamper in a boat even smaller than theirs. He held his paddle high and warned them: "Stay back! Got myself caught here between a mama gator and her babies...and boy she's angry!" He was trying to maneuver his boat clear of the area but kept getting trapped in the snarled vegetation on the bank.

Just then, the mother alligator surfaced. She was a whopper! Tabby watched in fascination and fear as the gator bumped the man's boat. Dad pointed out the nest on the shore. He held their boat steady, then frightened Tabby by announcing, "I'm going in to help...I don't think he'll ever get out of there."

Before Tabby could stop her father, he slapped her hand on the rudder, grabbed a line, and jumped over the side of the boat into the water. Tabby screamed.

Her father paid her no attention; his eyes were on the alligator on the other side of the swamper's boat. The gator was really angry now. Tabby could understand how a mother might feel about her babies being threatened, but she was petrified at the very sight of her dad in the water anywhere near something as large—and as toothy and upset—as this gator was.

As the gator headed for him, her dad shoved himself up on the swamper's boat, almost swamping it and tipping it over! Tabby screamed again. Just as the gator slammed her enormous jaws shut, her father tugged his feet into the boat. Quickly, he tied a line to the bow, then threw the other end to Tabby.

As she let go of the rudder and stood to catch the line, her boat rocked back and forth. *The gator turned and headed her way.*

CHAPTER TWELVE

THE TOOTH, THE WHOLE TOOTH, AND NOTHING BUT THE TOOTH

Tabby was too scared to scream. She missed grabbing the line and her father pulled it back in quickly, then threw again. "Catch it, Tabby!" he ordered. She could hear the fear in his voice.

Like slow motion, the line heaved out over the boat, up against the baby blue sky, then down, down, down it came...almost into her hand...but slipped against her fingertips. Just as it hit the edge of the boat, she reached out and grabbed it—her hand a split second away from the second snap of the big gator's angry jaws.

Tabby pulled the line so hard that she fell backwards onto the seat. She realized how easy it would be to fall out of the boat.

"Tie it off!" her father ordered.

Tabby looked around and found a place to tie the rope as tightly as she could. Then she sat down and held on to the boat seat as tightly as she could.

In just a moment, the professor tugged the boats together, hopped back into their boat, started the motor, which had gone dead, and began to pull the swamper's boat out of the elbow-shaped trap of swamp he was in.

As soon as space was free, the mother alligator—slapping her tail on the water—scooted ashore.

"Boy, I don't know how to thank you," said the swamper, as soon as they were clear of danger. "I been in these swamps fifty-some-odd years and never got myself in a fix like that. Much obliged. You, too, little swamp lady," he added. In spite of herself, Tabby blushed and smiled.

"No problem," said the professor. "But maybe you can help me, too."

Now, instead of looking grateful, the swamper looked suspicious. "How's that?" he asked.

"You know Mable Harper, over on that island she likes to call her Skullcracker Swamp?" the professor asked.

The swamper nodded *yes*.

"Well, she's as brave a swamper as I know. But now, she's scared. Says there's trouble in the swamp. Someone trying to scare her off her place. Maybe after something of value. You heard any rumors? Got any ideas?"

Tabby could tell from her father's voice that he really expected an honest answer in exchange for his helping the swamper out of the tight spot he had gotten himself into. In fact, Tabby wondered if the swamper was such a long-time pro, how he got himself into such a fix. She noted that he didn't talk *in the vernacular*, as Dad called it, like Aunt Mable did.

The man hesitated, rubbed his beard. Tabby noticed the shotgun lying in the floor of the boat. His blue eyes went steely gray.

"Welllll," he finally drawled, as if buying time to think. "I just came from Bugaboo Island. Did hear some rumors that some titanium deposits have been identified here-abouts. Some folks want to strip-mine in the swamp. Maybe she's in the way." He said this last sentence more as a threat than a concern for the old woman.

Then Tabby's dad surprised her by laughing, "Aw, probably nothing. Just a dotty old woman, you know. Probably got that Old Timer's disease," he said to the swamper.

The swamper laughed in relief. "Probably so," he agreed. "Well, I'll be moving on. Thanks again," he said, not particularly sincerely. "You, too, little lady," he added with a tip of his dirty felt hat. Tabby didn't blush or smile this time. She did not like the way the man looked at her.

Dad poled the boat so the man could get by, and without another word or wave, he moved on down the watercourse out of sight.

"Dad!" Tabby said, when the swamper was out of earshot. "Why did you say that about Mable? I know you don't believe she's lying or crazy or has Alzheimer's or anything."

Her father patted her arm, then when she looked like she might cry, slung his arm around her shoulder.

"Thanks," Tabby said with a nervous giggle, "but don't rock the boat, please." She glanced around for snakes or gators.

"Exactly!" said her Dad, turning her loose. "That's the point! I didn't want to rock the boat. I think that guy told me enough of the truth to keep me from being suspicious—he hoped!—and enough of a lie to keep me from detaining him further."

"I don't understand," admitted Tabby.

"There are valuable titanium deposits in the swamp," her father explained. "Even though this is a federally-protected refuge, that doesn't prevent

corporations from trying to get an exception, like maybe
purchasing mineral rights to strip-mine in the swamp,
which could destroy it forever."

Now Tabby was beginning to understand, just
a little. "So that guy could be a scout or a spy for
some company?"

"Maybe not that dramatic," her father said, but
Tabby thought he didn't sound so sure himself. "But I
doubt anyone seriously wanting to check out a place like
Skullcracker Swamp would let a little old lady like Mable
get in their way."

"He had a shotgun, Dad!" Tabby reminded him.

Her father surprised her by roaring with laughter.
"Well, so does Mable," he said. "And she's a crack shot!"

The professor turned the boat around.

"Aren't we still going to Bugaboo Island?"
Tabby asked.

"No," said her dad. "I think we will head back to
Mable's place. Somehow, I think she might be going to
have a visitor."

"Dad?" said Tabby in a quivering voice, as they
started in the opposite direction. It was only midafternoon and Tabby was surprised to realize that she
was disappointed to not get to go and see Bugaboo
Island. "Do you have a shotgun?"

The professor looked at his daughter. "No," he
said. "I don't believe in guns; you know that."

Suddenly, Old Man roared and the earth and the water and the air trembled.

CHAPTER THIRTEEN

FIRE!

As they headed back to Skullcracker Swamp, Tabby noticed a haze on the horizon. The air had a peculiar scent to it; it even stung her nose and eyes. Soon, they spotted smoke.

"What's that, Dad?" Tabby asked. She was surprised that even in the short time that she'd lived in the swamp with her father, she could quickly sense a change in the usually serene swamp setting.

Before the professor could answer, a boat roared up from Fargo. A ranger waved them down. The professor shut down the motor and gave the ranger a wave.

"Professor," the ranger said. "Just wanted to warn you...there's a brush fire that might get away from us. We hope to get it under control, but the wind may pick up this afternoon."

"Lightning strike?" the professor asked.

The ranger shook his head somberly. "No. It looks more like a careless camper who didn't put out their campfire."

"Well, that's too bad," said the professor, scanning the horizon. "How close to Aunt Mable's place?"

"Pretty far, right now, but, like I said, depending on the wind...." Before the ranger could finish his sentence, a breeze swirled around them.

"I'll get my radio on," said the professor. The ranger nodded and sped off.

"Is that dangerous, Dad?" Tabby asked. "A fire in a swamp sounds weird...I mean there's so much water."

Dad shook his head as he started the motor and headed on down the waterway. "A fire in the swamp's not so bad if it's caused by Mother Nature...a lightning strike, for example. Dry peat is very **combustible**. That kind of fire can clear out underbrush. In fact, this whole ecosystem is actually dependent on fire for its good health. But arson or carelessness is a different story; that can ruin things for everyone."

"And the animals and birds, too?" Tabby guessed. She imagined how frightened the swamp creatures would be to have to flee their homes in all the scary smoke.

"You, bet," said Dad. "A natural fire's not fun, but it's nature's way to help. A careless fire is stupid. And arson—well, that's a crime!"

Tabby watched her Dad's face. He seemed like a hawk, lifting his nose to check the wind, watching in all directions. She knew he was worried, because he made the boat go faster and they took turns at a steeper bank, spewing a spray of water behind them.

"Will Aunt Mable be OK?" Tabby asked, holding tight as the turns sent her side to side on the wet, slippery boat seat.

"She'll be OK," Dad promised.

But even as he said that, he pushed the throttle and made the boat go even faster.

CHAPTER FOURTEEN

THE
VISITOR

They skidded quickly over the water past prairies (that Dad called *per-rair-ees*). They swept past mounds, hammocks, and pine islands until they rounded a curve and came upon Skullcracker Swamp.

At first glance, Tabby thought Aunt Mable had started a roaring fire in the large stone fireplace. But Tabby quickly realized that the smoke she saw was coming from the wildfires in the swamp beyond the cabin.

"It looks so close, Dad!" she said to her father.

He nodded as he tied up the boat. "Mable!" he called loudly. "Mable!"

Tabby noted that her father took his field notebooks and shoved them into a metal container. He did the same with the specimens of flora and fauna he had collected so far today.

And then her dad did something that she had never heard him do before, not even in the swamp—he "hollered." It wasn't hollering like screaming, it was a deep sort of yodeling sound. In some ways, to Tabby, it sounded like a friendlier version of Old Man.

In a moment, they both heard a "holler" back.

"Something's wrong," said the professor. He stamped up the bank and "hollered" again. This time, no one responded.

"Get on the porch and stay there," he ordered his daughter. "I'm going around back; I'll be right back. Whatever happens, *don't move*!"

The tone in his voice made Tabby very afraid. She did not think that the fire was that close. Maybe her dad was worried that the man they had met this morning had paid Aunt Mable a visit. Maybe he had come to talk to her about giving up Skullcracker Swamp to the strip-miners. Maybe...well, Tabby didn't want to think about the possibilities! *Murder and mayhem,* she recalled Aunt Mable saying.

Quickly, she obeyed her father, and without a glance, he strode around behind the cabin. Tabby wondered how far he would go into the woods and swamp. She did not like being out here alone, mainly because she was beginning to realize that you were never really "alone" in the swamp.

As Tabby sat there, her chin cupped in her hands, she wondered how Aunt Mable could live in such an isolated place in such primitive conditions. No "911," thought Tabby. No ambulance to race to your aid. No rescue squad. No doctor. No nurse. Dad had told her how Indians once stopped bleeding from wounds by stuffing them with Spanish moss.

Tabby was so busy thinking to pass the time that she did not realize that she had a visitor herself. At first, she felt his presence, then she slid her eyes to the left, to the shadow at the edge of the pines.

At first it was just that—a shadow. Then as the breeze shifted the pine boughs, sunlight fell upon her visitor. Tabby now felt like "hollering" herself, and would have, had she not been so petrified to see the BEAR!

CHAPTER FIFTEEN

OLD BILL

Tabby struggled to not scream. Somehow, her instincts told her to sit as still as she could.

The bear was black as tar. He pretended (or at least that's what Tabby thought) to sniff and snip at some nearby gallberries. *Move or not move*, Tabby pondered desperately. She listened hard. She did not hear her dad anywhere around back. She did not hear Aunt Mable. She did not know if the cabin door was unlocked, in case she tried to make a run for it.

Let's see, she tried to remember: if you run from an alligator, you run in a zigzag pattern; if you run from a bear, you run...FAST! Or, do you not run at all? Tabby wished she had listened harder to her father's almost continuous "instructions" about the swamp as they had boated the waterways.

Suddenly, the question was a moot point—the bear stood up on his hind legs! Tabby could see a patch of white fur. She was frozen in fear. Maybe he was just trying to look big and tall and scary? No, she thought: he WAS big and tall and scary!

She willed herself not to scream. Just as she hunkered down inside to give herself the power to propel herself upwards and across the porch and—*hopefully*—through the front door of the cabin, a voice spoke softly.

"Stay still...very still." It was her father's voice. Out of the corner of her eye, she could see him in the bushes on the other side of the cabin. He held a shotgun—aimed straight at the bear.

The bear sniffed the air. He opened his mouth, revealing long, curved teeth. He shuffled a few steps and roared!

The very sound of his voice so nearby caused Tabby to tremble. She was not moving, but she was moving. She sat very still, but her arms and legs quivered.

"Do not move, Tabitha, do NOT move." The professor said this softly, and he did not move either. He kept himself hidden in the trees. But Tabby could

see the business end of the shotgun sticking out just a few inches from a sweetgum tree.

Suddenly, shockingly, another swamp character made an appearance: "Shoo-ee!" hollered Aunt Mable as she came around the corner of the cabin. "It's some kinda hot. A storm's a brewin' I tell ya."

When she spotted the professor with the shotgun from her back porch, and saw Tabby frozen in place on the porch, Aunt Mable immediately knew something was wrong. She looked and saw the large bear tumble to all fours. Instead of running, or freezing in place, Aunt Mable reached down and picked up some large stones and threw them at the bear!

"GET OUT OUTTA HERE, BILLY BEAR; GO ON NOW! GO GET YOU SOME HONEY AND LEAVE US ALONE!"

To Tabby's surprise, the bear turned and ran! He stopped once and glanced around as if his feelings were hurt. Aunt Mable threw another stone and hollered, and off the bear clomped into the forest.

The professor stepped out of the woods and lowered the gun. "Only a swamper's that brave!" he said to the spry old woman who had a satisfied look on her face.

"Or foolish!" answered Aunt Mable. "But I've run Old Bill off a number of times. He means me no harm. I guess the fire's got him nervous and roving. He won't be back today."

On the porch, Tabby sat with her mouth hanging open. "I think I might have wet my pants," she said.

When the adults laughed, Tabby asked, "Well, if he won't be back today...will he be back tomorrow?"

Aunt Mable shook her head slowly. "Not sure any of us will be back tomorrow. The wind's changed and the fire's a-rampaging this way; be here by dark."

CHAPTER SIXTEEN

THE HURRICANE

Tabby soon discovered that Aunt Mable's swamp-skill instincts, honed over time and experience, were very good. A ranger came by and confirmed that they should prepare to "evacuate the area." Tabby noticed that Aunt Mable just nodded, then went in her cabin and started to prepare dinner.

"You need to talk to her," the ranger told the professor. He had a funny sound in his voice, as if more than once he had warned a swamper of danger, only to be rebuffed.

"I will," Professor Flynn promised. "Any other news?"

The ranger looked tired and nervous. "Yes," he said. "If you've got a radio turn it on. That tropical storm that was supposed to have passed us by has done a doubletake and is headed directly for the swamp. Category two right now; forecast to be a three or four by nightfall."

When her father tried to ask more questions, the ranger brushed him off. "Sorry, sir, I've got a lot more folks to warn. Gotta go now. Just pack on up and get on out. I'd suggest any way but there." As he said this, he threw his arms in two different directions.

In her mind, Tabby added two more no-no routes...one into the dark swamp of gator holes...and the other where the bear had headed, who knows how far?

"Dad!" Tabby said, as soon as the ranger took off. "Isn't a Category Two or Three or Four what they call hurricanes?"

The professor nodded. "Those storms can change their minds and get stronger in a hurry. I'll get the radio on and see what I can hear."

Inside the cabin, Aunt Mable must have been listening because she thrust her swamp-haired head out the door and pumped her wrinkled fist in the air. "Bring it on!" she said. "The hurrycane can put out the fire.

See how that works?" she added to Tabby. The wink she gave her did nothing to make Tabby feel better.

"Mable," said the professor, in a most serious and earnest voice. "You know we need to leave. You know I have to get Tabby to safety. You need to come, too."

Aunt Mable just lurched back inside the cabin, letting the screened door slam behind her. "Not a'goin'," she said. "Can't go." Next, they heard the clatter of dishes.

"Dad! What are we doing to do?" Tabby asked. "I'm scared. We have to talk Aunt Mable into leaving, and right away!"

The professor sucked on his bottom lip as he thought. "I know, Tabby," he said. "But I can't kidnap her; she's stubborn as an old goat, and for all I know, she plans to meet her maker in this swamp. I just hope it's not tonight."

"DAD!" Tabby repeated. She did not like any talk about meeting-your-maker. She did not like the stinging in her eyes from the **encroaching** smoke. And she did not like the idea of a hurricane dumping enough water in the swamp to put the gators on the land, or huffing enough wind to shake down trees and the snakes on their branches. She thought to herself: *I'm leaving if I have to leave alone!* And then, Tabby began to cry.

CHAPTER SEVENTEEN

FIRE & WATER, WIND & RAIN

Her father grabbed her and crushed her to his chest. "Oh, Tabitha, please, please don't cry. You'll be OK; I promise I'll take care of you, no matter what happens. I'm your father."

In spite of herself, Tabby began to laugh, even as she wiped her nose with her tee shirt. Then she surprised herself by admitting, "Oh, Dad, I'm not worried about me. I'm worried about you and Aunt Mable. I couldn't bear to lose either one of you."

Just then Aunt Mable stuck her head back out on the porch. "Did you say bear? Is Old Bill back? I'll get that..."

"No, no, no," the professor assured her.

"Good," said the old woman. "Then in that case, dinner's ready."

Father and daughter looked at one another and burst out laughing. "There's a fire and a hurricane about to collide in Skullcracker Swamp and you're serving dinner?" the professor said.

Like the bear, Aunt Mable pretended her feelings were hurt. "Well, I don't know about you, but if tonight's my night, I might as well have a good meal first!" She disappeared back inside.

Dad and Tabby were no longer laughing. Tabby felt her stomach churn as she watched her Dad peer first over the cabin at the red, smoky sky...then turn to check the churning dark clouds filled with green centers and gold flashes of lightning.

The professor took his daughter by the shoulders and headed her inside the cabin.

"Dad," said Tabby. "In a hurricane, aren't you supposed to get in the basement?"

Before her father could answer, Aunt Mable blurted. "Honey, chile: the swamp IS the basement."

CHAPTER EIGHTEEN

A TOUGH DECISION

"Mable," said Dad. "We have to go, all of us, NOW—you know that." He had both palms pressed flat on the end of the rough hewn log dining table. He stared into the old woman's watery swamp-colored eyes.

For a moment there was silence. Tabby held her breath. Finally the old woman spoke. She spoke softly, gently. "Yes, Allistair, I know you do." She motioned at the large basket on the table, the thermos. "Why do you think I've packed this meal for you?"

It was not a question. Tabby knew that. She also knew that her father knew that. And, she also knew that she had never heard anyone call her father Allistair, his given name, before. Maybe Al, often professor, but never Allistair.

She figured that was like when an adult says a kid's name in full—"TABITHA LEE FLYNN!" her grandmother would scream, and she knew she was in big trouble, though she often did not know for what reason. Tonight Tabby knew there was big trouble, and she knew the reasons—fire and water.

But she did not know the half of the trouble until Aunt Mable allowed tears to come to her eyes. She took both their hands in hers. "Go on, now children. I was born in the swamp, and I'll die in the swamp. It's time and it's the way I want it. Besides, I'm not leaving Skullcracker Swamp—burnt black nor washed away—to the man I tracked today...the one who wants my land for the minerals that may be buried beneath it. I've dug many a year here and only ever found one thing: a skull. And just in case you need to know, I'm not afyeard, not one mite."

No one spoke. But Tabby was afraid, very afraid.

Finally, her dad asked, "What man? What did he look like? Where did you track him?"

"Tracked him to the edge of the swamp," said Mable. "Caught him taking some soil samples. He looked like a swamper, but he's no swamper! He's a

fake and bad news. If I leave, he will get my land. I know it, I just know it!"

Tabby and her father could see that the old woman was so distraught that it would be almost impossible to get her to leave with them. But Tabby knew that her dad would never leave the old woman behind.

Dad put his arm around Aunt Mable and lead her down the porch steps. With his eyes he told Tabby to move on ahead toward the boat. For a moment, Mable seemed confused. She did not seem to know if she was going or coming, so much to their surprise, she came along with them.

However, as they moved away from the cabin, the old woman suddenly seemed to realize what was happening. "I won't go! I won't go!" she kept repeating.

They were so focused on Aunt Mable that when they finally got to the water's edge, it was a moment before they realized the unbelievable: their boat was gone!

CHAPTER NINETEEN

STRANDED!

"Dad!" Tabby screamed. "Where's the boat?!"

Tabby looked up and down the waterway. The wind had increased so much that little whitecaps had formed even in this shallow, narrow water. The grasses were swaying, not gently, but heeled over like sails about to touch the water. The towering trees above them did the same. It was hard to tell the clouds from the smoke, they were so intermingled. And then Tabby realized something else—it was getting darker. Night was coming. Were they stranded? Doomed to spend the night trapped in a cabin under attack by the fire whipped to a frenzy by the wind and dry timber? Or would the hurricane bring a surge of water to cover the island completely?

"Tabby, look!" her father screamed over the noise of the wind. He pointed down the swamp.

Truly, Tabby was afraid to look. Perhaps he was trying to get her to see their boat, come loose from its mooring. Or was it another bear? A gator? The bad guy? But this was no time for cowardice.

Squinting into the swirl of smoke and storm, all Tabby could see was gray. Then suddenly, moving out of the gray mist toward them was a boat. In the boat was a ranger and a young boy.

"Over here!" Tabby screamed. "Over here!" she hollered louder.

The ranger, who had been about to turn his boat a different direction, looked up. "I see you!" he hollered back, and headed toward them.

When he got close, the boy jumped out and pulled the boat to shore. He did not tie up but held the line as if they would only be there a minute.

"I'm Ranger Ned Nelson. This is my son Gabby. Howdy, Miz Harper. If you guys need help, I can take you, but we gotta go now. Even then—"

The professor did not let the ranger finish his sentence. "Our boat got loose. We'll come with you— right now. Thanks," he added.

Gabby held out his hand and helped Tabby into the boat. She moved to the middle seat to make room for the others. The boat bobbed and swayed.

As the professor tried to help Aunt Mable into the boat, she acted like she would come along. Then, suddenly, she balked and began to weep. "I can't go, I just can't!" she wailed.

The ranger looked at the professor and the professor looked at the ranger. It amazed Tabby to see the two men communicate clearly without ever saying a word. Tabby thought adults were pretty interesting and amazing sometimes.

Ranger Nelson took Aunt Mable by the arm. "I promise we'll get you back, Miz Harper. I know about the bad guys. They can't fight fire and storm either. Come on with me, now, and we'll get to safety...then we'll get you back before anything bad can happen to your Skullcracker Swamp. I promise."

Tabby noticed that while the ranger spoke in firm, reassuring words, both he and her father were getting the woman in the boat and settled. The ranger wrapped a tarp around her. She seemed calm, or at least resigned.

When the adults were settled, Gabby jumped into the boat and tugged the line in after him. With a pole, he shoved them off the bank, then sat beside Tabby. "Hold on," he said. "It's gonna be a rough ride."

CHAPTER TWENTY

INTO THE STORM!

Sure enough, as the long boat sped through the water, it was a rough ride. The Okefenokee was now nothing like the sweet, serene swamp Tabby had witnessed in the past few days.

Wind and rain pummeled them. Neither bird nor animal was to be seen; through their keen natural instincts they had gone to safety as best they could. This small group of people was desperately trying to do the same, but would they be successful?

Tabby was shocked to see the ranger steer the boat toward the fire. The rain had not reached the fire yet, and so the flames seemed closer than ever, especially staring into the roaring wildfire at ground—or rather, water—level.

Suddenly, and with no warning, the ranger swept the air boat in a wide arc. A fishtail of water spewed upward. He made the elbow turn and now they headed into the storm.

Lightning crackled in the trees; thunder boomed overhead as loudly as Old Man, the ancient gator, had ever roared.

As they sped into the storm, they were blinded by the stinging water. But the ranger never slowed down. Tabby held tightly to the boat with one hand and even tighter to Gabby's arm with the other. "It'll be OK," she thought she heard him say to her. And then suddenly, the boat jolted to a stop, the motor quit, and it seemed they were under attack on all sides!

CHAPTER TWENTY ONE

RESCUE

The boat rocked fiercely. Hands grabbed at them. Despite the loudness of the storm, Tabby heard voices, faint, though they were in and around the boat.

"Get her out!" one cried.

"Tie it up!" screamed another.

"Let's move!" hollered another.

"There's not much time!" shrieked someone else.

Tabby felt the boat rock fiercely in the darkness. She felt things and people brush past her. Water washed in and soaked her feet. A loud CRACK! made her ears ring. The smell of **acrid** smoke stung her nostrils.

And then, suddenly, it was blindingly dark as someone swung a tarp over her head, and plucked Tabby from the boat. She felt herself pulled up high into the storm, then bounced and jounced as the person who carried her ran in big, giant leaps.

The next thing she heard was a loud BLAM! And when the tarp was yanked off of her head, she saw that they were all safe—inside a cabin lit by a kerosene lantern.

CHAPTER TWENTY TWO

SWAMP FROLIC REDUX

For a moment no one spoke. There was a lot of heavy breathing as everyone caught their breath. In the dark, smoke-filled air, the flickering lantern light made them all appear more like ghosts than humans.

Then there was an unmistakable laugh: "Lordy, lordy, I declare!" said Aunt Mable. "I've been in the swamp all my life and thought I'd seen everything. But tonight's a night for the history books."

Dad gave a big sigh. "Yes," he said. "This summer, I wanted Tabby to learn to love the swamp like I do." He came over and gave his wet, bedraggled daughter a big hug and a kiss. He looked her in the eyes. "But after tonight's adventure, I fear she'll give up the wild outdoors forever."

Tabby blinked and smiled. "Oh, Dad, don't give up on me...and I won't give up on—you know, gators and such."

That made the rangers who had rescued them laugh. "All in a day's work for us," said one.

"Just glad it's not everyday's work!" said another, and the rest nodded.

Just then Gabby came out of another room with an armload of warm, dry towels. "Anyone want a—" he began, but before he could finish his sentence, the towels disappeared from his arms.

Gabby grinned. "My Dad's got some soup on, too," he said.

Just then, Ranger Nelson came in from another room. "Been on the radio," he said. "Looks like the fire's been put out by the heavy rains. Hurricane's been downgraded to a tropical storm. I think we're out of the woods."

"What about Skullcracker Swamp?" the professor asked softly. Tabby knew he meant Aunt Mable's cabin and all her things—like the skull she'd dug up so long ago, likely as not, a former swamper from times past.

Ranger Nelson grinned. "About like Miz Harper here. Still there! Not goin' anywhere."

Gabby was serving the old woman a bowl of the steaming "swamp stew." Aunt Mable smiled. She was missing a tooth. "Reckon I never was. Reckon I never will." Her eyes twinkled beneath the swamp nest of hair. "And now," she added, "while we wait out the rest of the storm, cain't we have a bit of a frolic?"

Everyone laughed. Gabby tossed another log on the big fire one of the rangers had started in the fireplace. Another kerosene lantern was lit. Ranger Nelson pulled out a fiddle and another ranger pulled out a banjo. The frolic began!

As the men played a lively tune, Tabby got up and went and sat by the old woman. "And so, what *is* the secret of Skullcracker Swamp?" she asked.

Aunt Mable grinned. "The secret of the swamp is that the swamp always wins. The swamp's always right. Don't argue with no swamp. It gives and takes. You'd better give it respect and only take what it can **replenish**."

"And what about that skull?"

"That skull? Why that was the first Old Bill— the one that made the mistake of not running away from me!"

POSTLOGUE

PROFESSOR FLYNN

Professor Flynn hummed softly while plucking specimens for photographs for a new book on the Okefenokee Swamp. It was a warm, sunny spring day...the water was sweet and clear...the birds chirped merrily...and all seemed serene in this wild, wet, wonderful wonderland.

Suddenly, an air boat burst from a side creek. The professor groaned as a specimen fluttered into the water.

"Sorry," said the ranger. His name was Gabby Nelson. He was a young, handsome man, tan with rosy cheeks, slim and trim. "I'm really sorry, Professor Flynn," the ranger

repeated. He had a twinkle in his eye and gave the professor a big smile.

"If I forgive you, will you take me to dinner?" the professor asked, also with a twinkle in the eye and a smile. "And none of that 'chicken' that's really alligator—I fell for that once upon a time!"

The ranger smiled at Professor Tabitha Flynn, the new naturalist in the swamp. Although he'd just been a boy back then, he remembered her father. He remembered the night of the famous fire and storm, still talked about over campfires at night. After that, they'd both gone away to school, but now, here they were, both swampers.

"How about a big steak?" Ranger Nelson asked.

"Sounds like a great idea," said Tabby. "Maybe we could grill out over at Skullcracker Swamp?"

The ranger laughed. "You cooking, professor? Sounds pretty darn scary to me!"

THE END??

about the author

Carole Marsh is an author and publisher who has written many works of fiction and non-fiction for young readers. She travels throughout the United States and around the world to research her books. In 1979 Carole Marsh was named Communicator of the Year for her corporate communications work with major national and international corporations.

Marsh is the founder and CEO of Gallopade International, established in 1979. Today, Gallopade International is widely recognized as a leading source of educational materials for every state and many countries. Marsh and Gallopade were recipients of the 2004 Teachers' Choice Award. Marsh has written more than 50 Carole Marsh Mysteries™. In 2007, she was named Georgia Author of the Year. Years ago, her children, Michele and Michael, were the original characters in her mystery books. Today, they continue the Carole Marsh Books tradition by working at Gallopade. By adding grandchildren Grant and Christina as new mystery characters, she has continued the tradition for a third generation.

Ms. Marsh welcomes correspondence from her readers. You can e-mail her at fanclub@gallopade.com, visit carolemarshmysteries.com, or write to her in care of Gallopade International, P.O. Box 2779, Peachtree City, Georgia, 30269 USA.

built-in book Club
talk about it!

Questions for Discussion

1. What is a swamp?

2. Why are swamps important habitats?

3. Does it matter if swamps are destroyed by filling them in to build on or by digging them out for minerals, for examples?

4. What would living in a swamp be like for a family versus living on land?

5. How do you think Tabby changed over the course of this story?

6. Why do you think Professor Flynn liked working in the Okefenokee Swamp so much?

7. What is a botanist or a naturalist? Why is their work important?

8. Why did Aunt Mable not want to leave her
   Skullcracker Swamp?

9. Who looks out for the "rights" of swamps, the
   creatures who live there, and the people, if any,
   who live there?

10. Who are the "two" Professor Flynns in this story?

built-in book Club

bring it to life!

Activities to Do

1. Draw a picture of a swamp. Research to be as accurate as you can of the color of the water, the types of trees and flowers; be sure and add birds and animals. If this is a class project, you could also draw a large mural of a swamp, or stick your individual drawings together in a long row to create a larger "swamp scene."

2. Write a short play using as many of the old-timey Okefenokee "swamper" expressions as you can. Note: There are expressions in the story, in the glossary of this book, on our website (see the Tech Connects page in this book), and in the Teacher's Guide available for this book.

3. Learn about alligators! Do research or visit our website to learn many fascinating facts about alligators. Make a papier-mâché alligator, or draw alligator pictures.

4. Have a Swamp Frolic! Turn your classroom into a "swamp," dress as "swampers," use fiddles or other homemade musical instruments to have a Swamp Band, make a Swamp Stew (a recipe is on our website), and eat, dance, sing, and tell stories. Go to www.carolemarshmysteries.com for more info and resources.

5. Be a naturalist! Make a Swamp Scrapbook with cardboard, paper, and twine. Collect "specimens" you might find in a swamp and add them to your scrapbook along with your naturalists' notes!

Pretty darn scary
glossary

 acrid: a very strong, upleasant smell

addled: confused or crazy

 carnivorous: describing an animal that primarily eats meat

 combustible: able to catch fire and burn

 encroaching: intruding without permission

freshet: a sudden heavy rain that causes the creeks to overflow their banks

passel: a lot of something

 replenish: refill

somerset: somersault

tomes: books, usually large ones

Pretty darn Scary
Scavenger hunt

Check off items on this list by finding the items in the book, or by visiting the Okefenokee Swamp!

__1. The name of the swamp...and how it got its name!

__2. A list of the "parts" of a swamp.

__3. The color of the swamp's water.

__4. Learn one swamp "legend."

__5. List five "critters" that live in the swamp!

__6. List four kinds of birds that fly in the swamp!

__7. Name the scariest (to you!) animal that lives in the swamp.

__8. Define one new word you learned about a swamp!

__9. Tell one way that living in a swamp is different from living on land.

__10. What is "swamp gas"?

tech
Connects

Useful Websites to Visit

Check out these websites for more information about
the Okefenokee Swamp!

www.carolemarshmysteries.com for additional reproducible
activities, fact sheets, and more!

www.okefenokee.com for all kinds of interesting
information, including about alligators, Okefenokee
legends, and more!

www.fws.gov/okefenokee for the Okefenokee National
Wildlife Refuge's website, which has a great map of
the swamp!

www.wacona.com for the Wacona Elementary School
website. This school is in Waycross, Georgia–right
near the Okefenokee!

enjoy this excerpt from...

The Ghosts of
Pickpocket
Plantation

by Carole Marsh

#1

CHAPTER ONE

his name was telesphore

HIS NAME WAS TELESPHORE. He had no idea why his grandmother had named him that. His grandmother had had to name him because his mother had died giving birth to him. His father was nowhere to be found. No name had been selected, not even hinted at, much less batted about from some charming book of baby names. So his grandmother named him Telesphore. Thank goodness his friends called him Terry. But somehow, deep underneath, he felt like Telesphore, a name that seemed auspicious, but also a burden. But he couldn't think of that now. Now he had to think of snakes.

Water moccasins were part and parcel of the peat bog swamp that surrounded Pickpocket Plantation. So were alligators. Mosquitoes the size of saucers. Wild turkeys. And, rarely, a wild boar.

"Watch where you s.....t......e......p," Terry reminded himself. His Aunt Penelope had lent him a beat-up old

pair of hightop, lace-up boots, but he figured a
diamondback rattler's fangs could easily pierce right
through the leather as if it were butter. Terry realized
that he had involuntarily squiggled his feet so far back
up into his shoes that his toes were cramping. "Step
carefully," he whispered to himself.

Terry wondered how anyone had ever gotten
anything done going tippy-toe around the enormous
plantation acreage. "Shoot," he said aloud, again to
himself, "I will just stomp along like brave Huck Finn
might have done and take what comes." As he
walked more willfully, he tried to recall if Tom
Sawyer and Huck Finn had been more brave, or
cowardly. Either way, they were on the Mississippi
River, and Terry did not think alligators the length of
small cars had ever worried them, except perhaps in
their imaginations.

In Terry's imagination, he was scouting out
Pickpocket as it must have been in the days of the
Yamacraw Indians, or in the painful era of plantation
slavery, or during the wily time of the Civil War (the War
of Northern Aggression, as some old-time southerners
still called it), or some other time of historic excitement.
But, really, Terry knew in his heart that he was just
trying not to be bored.

Or scared. After all, didn't Aunt Penelope say that
the Saturday *Savannah Pilot* recently featured a story

about a fisherman poling his skiff through some snarled morass of wetland weeds getting his foot chomped off by a gator?

"*Step carefully, Terry...*

c   a   r   e   f   u   l   l   y."

WRITE YOUR OWN MYSTERY!

Make up a dramatic title!

You can pick four real kid characters!

Relect a real place for the story's setting!

Try writing your first draft!

Edit your first draft!

Read your final draft aloud!

You can add art, photos or illustrations!

Share your book with others and send me a copy!

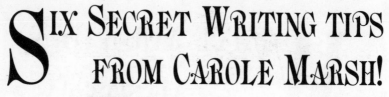

Six Secret Writing tips from Carole Marsh!

Non-fiction is factual!

1. Make up good titles – wild and crazy is good!

2. Use strong verbs – action verbs with pizzazz!

3. Edit your work to make it better!

4. Use your own special "voice" to make your work unique!

5. Use a thesaurus and dictionary to find the words that mean what you want to say!

Fiction is made up!

6. Don't worry about rules – use your imagination and have fun!